GIFT OF

John Warren Stewig

Carthage

The First Voyage OF CHRISTOPHER COLUMBUS 1492

BARRY SMITH

VIKING

How to use this book

Christopher Columbus left Spain on 11 May 1492 and returned to Spain 14 March 1493. This book traces, step by step, his voyage to America and back. On each page, where relevant, you will find a map which shows you the position of his ships at that particular point in the voyage. Using these maps you can trace for yourselves the complete journey of Columbus on the large fold-out map at the end of the book (use the grid lines and references to make this easier) and see his historic voyage spread out before you.

VIKING

Published by the Penguin Group
Penguin Books Ltd, 27 Wrights Lane, London W8 5TZ, England
Penguin Books USA Inc., 375 Hudson Street, New York, New York 10014, USA
Penguin Books Australia Ltd, Ringwood, Australia
Penguin Books Canada Ltd, 10 Alcorn Avenue, Toronto, Ontario, Canada M4V 3B2
Penguin Books (NZ) Ltd, 182-190 Wairau Road, Auckland 10, New Zealand

Penguin Books Ltd, Registered Offices: Harmondsworth, Middlesex, England

First published 1992
1 3 5 7 9 10 8 6 4 2

Text and illustrations copyright © Barry Smith, 1992

The moral right of the author/illustrator has been asserted

Filmset in Bembo

Printed in Hong Kong by Imago Publishing Ltd

A CIP catalogue record for this book is available from the British Library

ISBN 0–670–84051–3

Long ago, in Palos in Spain, there was a sailor who needed a job. So he found a sea captain who was looking for men to sail his ships.

7

LISBON

PALOS

d

"My name is Christopher Columbus," said the sea captain. "I've hired three ships to sail westwards to find the island of Cipangu, the land of Cathay, and lots of treasure."

"He's crazy," thought the sailor. "But I do need the job."
"Goodbye, and good luck, dear," said his mother.
"Goodbye, Mother," said the sailor.

THE CANARY ISLES

The three ships sailed south by west to the Canary Islands where supplies were loaded and the ships fitted for their long sea voyage.

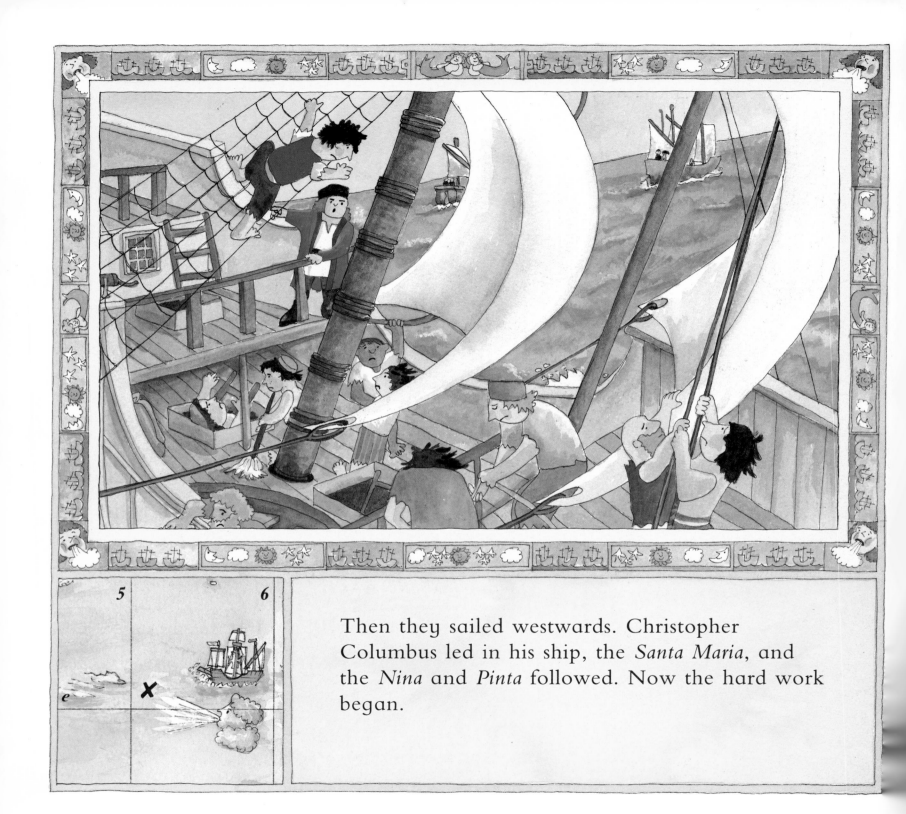

Then they sailed westwards. Christopher Columbus led in his ship, the *Santa Maria*, and the *Nina* and *Pinta* followed. Now the hard work began.

4   5

ATLANTIC OCEAN

✗

e

f

The days passed. The sailor soon grew tired of eating nothing but hard biscuits, garlic, onions and beans, and of sleeping on the cramped deck. "But I did need the job," he thought.

There were no maps to guide them. The sailor was scared. The crew grumbled and talked of mutiny.

They sailed onwards for over thirty days and nights. "Where in the world are we?" thought the sailor.

At last, one evening, a gun boomed out.
Land Ahoy!
"Well, we've arrived," said Christopher Columbus.
"Is this Cipangu — or Cathay?" asked the sailor.

"Er, near one of them, I think," said Christopher Columbus.
"We'll have to explore to find out."
"And where's all the treasure you promised us?"
asked the captain of the *Pinta*.
"I'm off to look somewhere else."

Many days passed as the sailors explored the new world they had found. Then one night, as everyone slept, the *Santa Maria* ran aground on a coral reef and was wrecked.

"Just our luck," thought the sailor.

The crew and all their supplies were rescued by the *Nina*.
"But one boat isn't big enough to take us all home," said Christopher
Columbus. "Some of you will have to stay here."
"Not me," thought the sailor. "I only came because I needed a job."

Houses were built for those who wanted to stay, and the *Pinta* returned to join the *Nina* for the homeward voyage.

The ships sailed north and at first the journey went well.

Then they sailed east. Dark clouds gathered and the weather began to change.

4   5

d

A terrible storm struck. The *Nina* and *Pinta* struggled against fierce winds, crashing waves, and thunder and lightning.

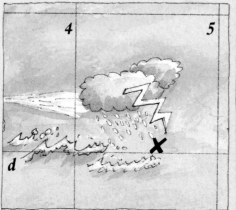

Christopher Columbus ordered the sailor to throw a sealed cask overboard containing the story of their adventures.

"Perhaps *someone* will find it," he said.

They lost sight of the *Pinta* in the second day of the storm. "Where in the world are we?" thought the sailor.

THE AZORES

But at last Christopher Columbus saw ahead a familiar coastline. They had come to the Portuguese islands of the Azores. The people did not like Spain or Spanish ships and Christopher Columbus had an argument with the Governor, but they did give the sailors food and helped them with their repairs.

They set sail again north by east.
"Perhaps we'll soon be home," thought the sailor.
But they ran into another storm and had to
shelter again in a Portuguese port near Lisbon.

6 7

c

X

LISBON

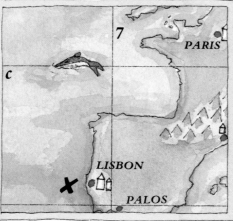

7

PARIS

c

LISBON

PALOS

"We won't be welcome here either," thought the sailor. Then a message came from the King of Portugal himself to say he wanted to see them. "Well done, Christopher Columbus," he said. "My congratulations to the crew."

He allowed them to leave for Spain right away.
"Home at last!" thought the sailor as they sailed for Palos.

LISBON

PALOS

7

d

As they arrived in port everybody cheered. The *Pinta* arrived later that same day.

"Mother! I'm home!"

Christopher Columbus and his crew went to visit the King and Queen of Spain to tell of their voyage and collect their reward.

"What about my pay?" the sailor asked Christopher Columbus.

"What about a medal instead?" suggested the King and Queen.

"Did you enjoy yourself?" asked the sailor's mother.
"Not really," said the sailor. "But I did need the job."

Christopher Columbus became the Admiral of the Ocean Sea and a respected seaman, and went on three more voyages to the New World. It seems likely that he never realized that what he thought was Cipangu (Japan) and Cathay (China) was actually the great continent and islands of the Americas. The world was a much bigger place than he imagined. He never did find any treasure either!